Some words
about piggy banks:

"Coink!!!"

An empty piggy bank

"No, I don't have any gold bars
I don't need."

Governor of the Bank of England

"Money doesn't grow on me."

A tree

"Or me!"

Another tree

"Aaaargh! You got me!"

Zombie mermaid

"I'll give you 5p for your roller blades."

A very annoying boy

More Daisy adventures!

DAISY AND THE TROUBLE WITH NATURE

DAISY AND THE TROUBLE WITH LIFE

DAISY AND THE TROUBLE WITH ZOOS

DAISY AND THE TROUBLE WITH GIANTS

DAISY AND THE TROUBLE WITH KITTENS

DAISY AND THE TROUBLE WITH CHRISTMAS

DAISY AND THE TROUBLE WITH MAGGOTS

DAISY AND THE TROUBLE WITH COCONUTS

DAISY AND THE TROUBLE WITH BURGLARS

DAISY AND THE TROUBLE WITH VAMPIRES

DAISY AND THE TROUBLE WITH CHOCOLATE

DAISY AND THE TROUBLE WITH SCHOOL TRIPS

DAISY AND THE TROUBLE WITH SPORTS DAY

JACK BEECHWHISTLE: ATTACK OF THE GIANT SLUGS

JACK BEECHWHISTLE: RISE OF THE HAIRY HORROR

Kes Gray

DAISY

and the trouble with

PIGGY BANKS

RED FOX

RED FOX

UK | USA | Canada | Ireland | Australia
India | New Zealand | South Africa

Red Fox is part of the Penguin Random House group of companies
whose addresses can be found at global.penguinrandomhouse.com.

www.penguin.co.uk
www.puffin.co.uk
www.ladybird.co.uk

Penguin
Random House
UK

First published 2015
This edition published 2020

001

Character concept copyright © Kes Gray, 2015
Text copyright © Kes Gray, 2015
Illustration concept copyright © Nick Sharratt, 2015
Interior illustrations copyright © Garry Parsons, 2015
Cover illustrations copyright © Garry Parsons, 2020

Set in VAG Rounded Light 15pt/23pt
Printed in Great Britain by Clays Ltd, Elcograf S.p.A.

A CIP catalogue record for this book is available from the British Library

ISBN: 978-1-782-95972-4

All correspondence to
Red Fox, Penguin Random House Children's
One Embassy Gardens, 8 Viaduct Gardens
London SW11 7BW

MIX
Paper from
responsible sources
FSC® C018179

Penguin Random House is committed to a
sustainable future for our business, our readers
and our planet. This book is made from Forest
Stewardship Council® certified paper.

To Garry, Duncan, Codie and Kyle

CHAPTER 1

The **trouble with piggy banks** is they're nearly always empty.

Plus whenever there is anything inside them, it's never enough to buy the things you really want. If piggy banks were full when people gave them to you, you could just open them up, take the money out and buy all the important things you need to buy, like really squirty things.

Trouble is, piggy banks aren't full of money when you get them. They are empty. They are full of a big fat nothingness that you can't spend on squirty things or things that don't even squirt. Or light up. Or make really cool noises. Which isn't my fault!

My mum says I was about a year old when I got my piggy bank from my nanny and grampy for Christmas. I didn't ask for a piggy bank – they just gave it to me. It's been empty ever since.

There have been times when I put a little bit of money in.

But the **trouble with putting money in a piggy bank** is, as soon as you put it in, you want to get it out.

Because as soon as you hear your money land inside the piggy's tummy, you realize you suddenly need it again.

The **trouble with suddenly needing your money again** is piggy banks are too easy to open.

Because all you have to do is turn them upside down, pull the little round stopper out of their tummy and shake the money out through the hole.

Which makes it really easy to spend and really difficult to save.

If you ask me, piggy banks shouldn't have little round stoppers in their tummies. If they didn't, they would be much better for saving actual money in. Trouble is, they do. So I don't save. Because my piggy bank won't let me save.

CHAPTER 2

Have you ever seen something that you really, really want but can't have, because you haven't got any money to buy it with? It happens to me all the time. Like when the ice-cream van drives down my street and the music makes me want a lolly. Or when my mum takes me to the post office and makes me stand by the sweets while we are waiting to buy some stamps. Or when I walk past a toy shop, or a gadget shop, or a toy shop that sells gadgets or a gadget shop that sells toys. Or it could be when my best friend totally gets given the best present in the absolute whole wide world and then brings it round to my house straight away because she absolutely totally can't wait to show it to me.

That's what happened to me two Saturday afternoons ago. I was sitting on the lawn in my front garden, training ants, when I suddenly heard the weirdest and coolest noise. It was a bit like an alien crossed with a chipmunk crossed with a gargling frog.

The **trouble with aliens crossed with chipmunks crossed with gargling frogs** is you're not exactly sure what to do when you hear one.

But it was OK because when I looked up, I realized it wasn't an alien or a chipmunk or a gargling frog, it was Gabby. She had come round to play with me . . . wait for it . . . on a brand-new micro-scooter . . . double wait for it . . . that didn't just do

alien-chipmunk-gargling-frog noises while it was scooting . . . triple wait for it . . . it flashed all over like a Christmas tree . . . and . . . fourpoople wait for it . . . squirted actual water just like a water pistol as well!!!!!

I didn't know about the squirting water bit until I ran over to my front gate for a closer look. That's when Gabby got me – all down my front!

"SURRENDER OR DROWN!" she laughed, pointing her handlebars at me, pushing the squirter button and then chasing me down my garden path.

Her brand-new micro-scooter was awesome! In fact, it was better than awesome. It was immense! (Immense is everyone's new word at school. You should use it as well.)

"My dad bought it for me!" said Gabby. "Isn't it immense?" (Gabby goes to the same school as me.) "He got a promotion at work and he bought it for me as a present because now he earns more money! And he gets a new car!"

I'd seen micro-scooters before. In fact, micro-scooters have been around for ages where I live. But I'd never seen one like this!

Gabby said it was the future of micro-scooters, which meant it was the very latest type of micro-scooter money could buy.

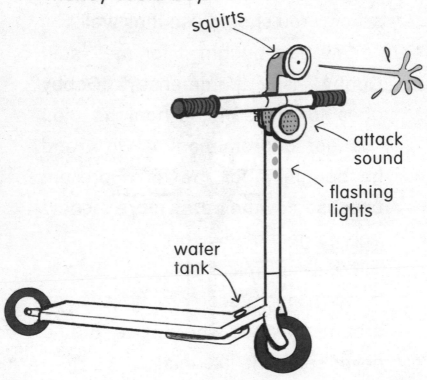

squirts

attack sound

flashing lights

water tank

It had three buttons you could push. The first one did the lights. The second one did the sounds. And the third one did the squirts!

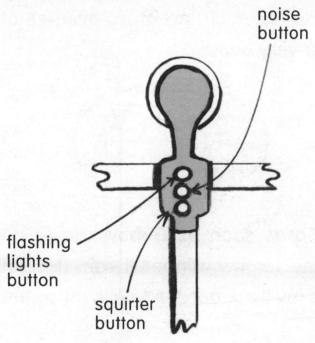

noise
button

flashing
lights
button

squirter
button

The **trouble with seeing your best friend on an immense squirting micro-scooter** is it makes you absolutely desperate to have an immense squirting micro-scooter of your very own.

So as soon as Gabby had to go home for her dinner, I ran straight into my back garden to ask my mum.

CHAPTER 3

"MUM, MUM!" I shouted, opening the kitchen door and leaping out into my back garden.

"WILL YOU BUY ME A SQUIRTING MICRO-SCOOTER JUST LIKE GABBY'S?"

The **trouble with waking my mum up when she's sunbathing** is it's better to do it quietly rather than shout.

"YOU SHOULD SEE HOW FAR A SQUIRTING MICRO-SCOOTER CAN SQUIRT!" I said. "YOU SHOULD SEE HOW MUCH A SQUIRTING MICRO-SCOOTER LIGHTS UP! PLEASE WILL YOU BUY ME ONE! PLEASE, PLEASE!!!"

At first I thought my mum was

going to say yes straight away, but when she took off her sunglasses and pulled a funny face, I began to have my doubts.

"Is it Christmas Day, Daisy," she said, "or is it a summer's day?"

"Summer," I said.

"Is it your birthday today, Daisy?" she said. "Or is your birthday in February?"

"February," I said.

"Then you know the answer to

your question, don't you," she said, putting her sunglasses back on and lying back down on the sun lounger.

The **trouble with knowing the answer to a question but not actually hearing it** is it makes you not want to give up.

"PLEEEEEEAAAASE!" I said. "Gabby's dad bought her a squirting micro-scooter without it being Christmas or her birthday, so why can't you?"

"Because we don't have the money that Gabby's mum and dad have, Daisy. I wish we did."

"But the squirts are immense!" I said. "And the noises and flashing lights are immense too!!"

"I'm sure the price is immense too," said my mum. "Have you asked Gabby how much a squirting micro-scooter costs?"

"Yes," I said, "and I know which shop you can buy them from."

"And?" said my mum.

"And what?" I said.

"And how much money are we talking?"

"Only £99.99," I said.

"In that case," said my mum, "the sooner you start saving, the better."

CHAPTER 4

When I rang Gabby to tell her that I was going to be getting a squirting, flashing, gargling micro-scooter of my very own, she sounded as excited as me!

Trouble is, then I had to tell her that it might be a while before I actually got it because my mum was making me save up to buy it myself.

"Oh," said Gabby, in a not-so-excited voice. "How much more money will you need to save up?"

"£99.99," I said.

When Gabby found out that I didn't have any money in my piggy bank at all, she said that I definitely wouldn't be able to buy one that day.

Which I already knew.

Then she told me that £99.99

was actually a lot of money to have to save up.

Which I already knew.

Then she told me that £99.99 was almost £100.

Which I already knew.

Then she told me it was only a penny less than £100.

Which I already knew.

Then she told me it was 9,999 pennies, if you said it in pennies and not pounds.

Which I didn't know, but didn't want to know either because now it sounded like I had even more money to save up.

"How much pocket money does your mum give you every week?" asked Gabby.

"50p," I said. "But I've already spent it."

"Have you got any rich relatives?" asked Gabby.

"I've got a nanny and grampy," I said, "but they bought me a piggy bank with no money in it, so I guess they must be poor."

"In that case," said Gabby, "there's only one thing you can do."

"What's that?" I asked.

"Chores," said Gabby.

"What are chores?" I asked.

"Jobs around the house," said Gabby, "like cleaning and washing-up and hoovering. If you do some chores, your mum could pay you for every chore you do."

"Really?" I said, getting quite excited.

"Really, really," smiled Gabby.

It was the best news I had heard all day.

"MUM! MUM! MUM," I shouted, racing back into the garden and waking her up again. "Will you pay me to do some chores?"

At first I wasn't sure what my mum was going to say, because I thought she might be grumpy after being woken up

twice. But I was wrong.

"Chores, eh?" she said. "I like the sound of that."

"When can I start?" I asked.

"As soon as you like," smiled my mum.

"And what will I get paid?" I asked.

"That, Daisy," said Mum, "will all depend on how well you do each chore."

CHAPTER 5

The **trouble with chores** is they are really hard work. Especially hoovering.

After I'd eaten my dinner on Saturday, Mum said I could start earning some money by hoovering the lounge. She got the hoover out, plugged it in and said that she would

come and inspect the carpet after
she had finished clearing the dinner
things away.

Trouble is, when she came back
into the lounge, I was hoovering an
orange.

I hadn't actually started off
hoovering an orange. I had started
off hoovering the carpet, but after
about twelve pushes I got a bit bored.

The **trouble with being bored** is
it makes you want to find out how
powerful a hoover suck can be.

Which is why I ended up hoovering the fruit bowl instead.

The **trouble with fruit bowls** is they have all kinds of fruits that you can try to suck up, like oranges, apples and bananas.

I was a bit worried that a banana might go all the way up the hoover pipe so I decided to try an orange first, because oranges are fatter.

And guess what? It worked!

The hoover pipe didn't just stick to the orange, it actually picked the orange up! I could pick up an actual orange with my actual hoover pipe, wave it around and everything! And make some really immense sucking, whining, hoovering noises at the same time!

The **trouble with immense sucking, whining, hoovering noises** is, if your mum hears them, she'll come and see what you are doing.

I was given a different chore to do after that.

The **trouble with washing the dishes** is, if you've had sausages and mash for dinner, then you need an immense amount of suds. Which is why I squeezed a full bottle of washing-up liquid into the bowl.

I didn't do it when my mum was in the kitchen. At first I only used a little bit. But after she'd gone upstairs to change the sheets on the beds, I realized how hard mashed potato was to get off.

The **trouble with realizing how hard mashed potato is to get off** is you don't have any choice really.

I thought I was doing a really good job of washing up the dishes, but when my mum came back downstairs and into the kitchen, she went loopy.

"HOW MUCH WASHING-UP LIQUID HAVE YOU USED?!" she shouted.

"IT LOOKS LIKE A CAR WASH IN HERE!"

I was given a different chore to do after that.

The **trouble with car washing** is ours is a really old car. So however much you wash it, it still looks rusty and old.

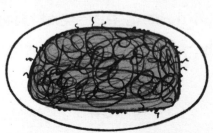

Which is why I decided to use a metal scouring pad instead of a sponge.

The **trouble with using a metal scouring pad** is metal scouring pads don't just rub dirt and rust off.

They rub actual paint off as well. And they make swirly shapes.

When Mum came out to do an inspection, I hadn't even noticed I was making swirly shapes all over the car, so it can't have been that bad. It was only when our neighbour, Mrs Pike, lent Mum her hosepipe to do the rinsing that the swirly shapes started to show up.

"LOOK AT THOSE SCRATCHES, DAISY! LOOK AT THOSE SCRAPES!" Mum shouted. "IT'S A CAR, NOT AN ICE RINK!"

When I told her that I couldn't actually see any swirly shapes or

scrapes on the car, she didn't believe me.

Then, when I asked her how much I was going to get paid, she went the colour of tomato sauce.

My next chore was getting ready for bed.

CHAPTER 6

Going to bed early on Saturday night was actually really handy, because it gave me some serious time to think of some serious ways of making some serious money.

Once I'd put my pyjamas on and got into bed, I began to have loads of money-making ideas. Trouble is, I wasn't sure if any of them would work.

The **trouble with opening a zoo** is, if you're going to charge people to come in to look at animals, you really need to have lots of animals for them to look at.

I could only think of two animals –

Mrs Pike's cat, Tiptoes, and my friend Dylan's snake, Shooter. Plus I wasn't very sure if Mrs Pike and Dylan would even lend them to me.

The **trouble with starting a pet hairdresser's** is I'm only allowed to cut things with the red scissors.

Plus I'm not sure my mum would let me use the hoover again, which means I wouldn't have anything to suck all the pet hairs up after I'd cut them, even if I got the red scissors to actually cut.

The **trouble with becoming a gold miner** is there aren't any gold mines in my street.

The **trouble with winning the lottery** is my mum always buys the wrong tickets.

And the **trouble with inventing a new invention that everyone in the world would want to buy** is I couldn't think of anything to invent. Apart from loom bands, but they've already been done.

When my mum came upstairs to say goodnight, I thought she was going to go on and on about washing-up liquid, and sucking up oranges, and scouring pads, but she didn't.

Instead of telling me off again, she gave me 50p for trying. Even if I hadn't tried very well.

She told me that when she was my age there were loads of things she wanted her mum and dad to buy her that her mum and dad couldn't afford, like the latest bike and the latest record and the latest clothes and the latest tortoise.

"Daisy, you do know that if I could afford to give you the money to buy a new scooter, I would, don't you?" said my mum.

"Yes," I said.

"And you do know that money

doesn't grow on trees, don't you?" she asked.

"Yes," I said.

"And you do know that birthdays and Christmases wouldn't feel half as special if children were bought presents all the time, don't you?"

"Not sure," I said.

"Well, you should be sure," said Mum.

"Howsabout," I said, suddenly having the best idea of my life. "Howsabout, if you give me all the money I need to buy an immense scooter right now, and I don't have any presents for my next three birthdays. OR Christmases!!! I only need another £99.49! . . . You can give it to me in a cheque . . . Or coins . . . Or notes. Or notes and coins. Or coins and notes. Whatever is easiest for you – I really, really, honestly don't mind! Plus, I promise never to clean the car again, or wash up, or hoover, or do any chores around the house again EVER!"

"Goodnight, Daisy," said Mum.

CHAPTER 7

When Gabby came round on Sunday morning, she didn't just bring her squirting micro-scooter, she brought her piggy bank too!

"You can have all the money inside!" she said, shaking her piggy bank and making it jingle. "I don't know how much there is, but you can have every penny I've got if you want it!"

At first I didn't know what to say. I mean, I knew Gabby was my best friend, but this was the kindest and bestest thing she had ever done for me in the world.

"Quick, bring your scooter indoors!" I said, before she changed her mind.

"Am I allowed to bring my scooter indoors?" asked Gabby.

"It's OK. My mum's in bed," I said. "She always has a lie-in on a Sunday morning."

As soon as Gabby knew that the coast was clear, she lifted her scooter over the front step and drove it into the lounge.

"Are there any £10 notes in there?" I asked as Gabby turned her piggy bank upside down.

"Just coins," said Gabby, pulling out the stopper in the piggy's tummy and giving it a shake.

"Here's one!" she said as the first coin fell onto the sofa. "Here's another one!" she smiled as another coin fell into my hand.

One by one, coin by coin, a pile of money began to build up on the sofa.

"Here's a big one!" Gabby said as a 50p bounced off her knee.

"My mum gave me one of those

last night for doing some chores!" I said.

"Now you've got two!" said Gabby. "Now you've got three!" she laughed as another 50p plopped out of the piggy bank and onto her lap.

"How much do you reckon there is?" I said, arranging the coins in different piles.

"Start counting!" said Gabby, giving the piggy bank one last shake to make sure there was no money left inside.

The **trouble with counting up piggy-bank money** is it's easy to lose count, especially if Gabby starts taking money from the piles you've already counted. Doubly especially if three of the coins are foreign.

The **trouble with foreign coins** is they don't speak the same language.

"How much is one EURO worth in English money?" I asked.

"I don't know," said Gabby.

"How much is a UNITED STATES OF AMERICA CENT worth?" I asked.

"Less than a EURO, I think," said Gabby.

"And what about two RANDS?" I asked.

"There's no such thing as RANDS, is there?" asked Gabby.

"Well, that's what it says on here," I said, holding up a silver-coloured coin with a picture of an antelope on it.

When we turned the coin over, we saw that it was speaking South African.

"It's got to be worth quite a lot if it's got an antelope on it," I said.

"Oh my gosh!" said Gabby, clapping her hand to her mouth and bouncing up and down on the sofa.

"Oh my gosh what?" I said, grabbing our English money as it started to slide off the cushions.

"What if it's a spelling mistake?" said Gabby. "What if instead of it saying RANDS it's meant to say GRANDS! Do you know how much a GRAND is, Daisy?!"

"No," I said.

"IT'S 1,000 ENGLISH POUNDS!"

"1,000 ENGLISH POUNDS!" I gasped.

"So if it's TWO GRANDS, it could be worth . . ."

"2,000 ENGLISH POUNDS!" squealed Gabby.

"I'm going to wake Mum!" I said, racing out of the lounge and leaping up the stairs.

CHAPTER 8

The **trouble with waking Mum again** is you need a really good reason to do it. Especially on a Sunday morning.

Trouble is, I thought I had 2,000 good reasons.

"MUM! MUM!" I said, charging into her bedroom with the antelope coin and shaking her as hard as I could.

"Is this two RANDS or two GRANDS?"

The **trouble with shaking my mum as hard as I could** is that when she opens her eyes, her eyeballs kind of roll the wrong way. Which is really weird. And a bit scary.

"Is what what??!?" she said, sitting up in bed and rubbing her eyes.

"Is this coin worth two RANDS or two GRANDS?" I asked. "Because if it's worth two GRANDS, I can buy a squirting micro-scooter right this very morning! And I can give you your 50p back!"

Once my mum had stopped rubbing her eyes, I gave her the coin with the antelope on to look at.

"It's two rands," she sighed.

"How much is that worth in English money?" I asked.

"About half a p, I should think," said my mum.

"What, even with an antelope on it?" I said. "The picture of an antelope must be worth at least 25p!"

"Even with an antelope on it," she said, sliding down under the covers again and going back to sleep. "And it's not an antelope, it's an eland."

When I got back to the lounge and told Gabby that it wasn't a spelling mistake, it was two rands, she looked as disappointed as I felt.

"You've got £2.76," she said, pointing to the money she had piled up on the sofa. "A lot of the coins were pennies and 5ps."

"Does that include the 50p my mum gave me yesterday?" I asked.

"Uh-huh," said Gabby gloomily.

The **trouble with taking £2.76 away from £99.99** is it looks easy unless you actually have to do it.

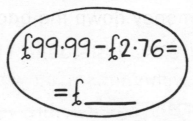

£99.99 − £2.76 =

= £ _____

Once we'd found my mum's calculator we worked out that I still needed to find another £97.23 before I could buy an actual squirting scooter just like Gabby's.

£97.23!

Where was I going to get that from!?

"Have you looked down the back of your sofa?" said Gabby. "There's always money down the back of our sofa at home. It falls out of people's pockets without them knowing."

"Really?!" I gasped, throwing away the little cushions and then heaving the two big fat sofa cushions onto the floor.

But I was wasting my time. The only things I managed to find were a paperclip, half a peanut, some crumbs and some fluff. Which aren't worth anything. Not even to a flea.

"Maybe some money has gone right down the back of your sofa and completely out of reach," said Gabby.

"What, you mean more 'underneath' the sofa than 'down the back'?" I asked.

"I guess so," said Gabby.

The **trouble with the underneath of sofas** is they are covered with material too. Which means if you lie on your back, crawl underneath and look up, you still can't see if anything has fallen down the back.

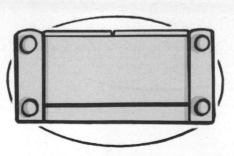

"I'll get some scissors," I said.

The **trouble with scissors** is I'm only allowed to use the red ones.

Trouble is, there is no way the red scissors would ever have been able to cut through the material underneath of the sofa.

Luckily, my mum was still asleep. So I used the big scissors from the kitchen drawer instead.

Trouble is, even when I'd cut all the way along the back and down both

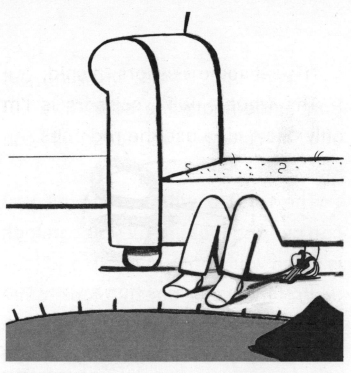

sides, I still didn't find any money. All I found was a piece of fingernail, loads more crumbs and fluff, plus a piece of cheese-and-onion crisp (I knew it was cheese and onion because it fell into my mouth when I was cutting).

"I give up," I said, crawling out from underneath the sofa. "I've cut all I can cut. And I've looked all I can look."

The **trouble with cutting all you can cut and looking all you can look** is when you stand up again and look down, the sofa doesn't look quite the same. Because after you've done your cutting, a big flap of material will be hanging down.

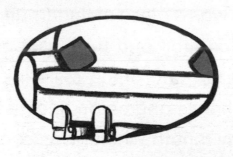

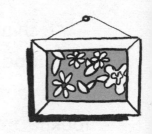

"I think you need to get some sellotape," said Gabby, with a bit of a nervous face.

The **trouble with sellotape** is it's all right for sticking bits of paper together, but it doesn't really work on the underneath of sofas. Which meant the flap kept falling down again.

"I think you should get some nails," said Gabby, looking even more nervous.

The **trouble with nails** is, once you've got some out of the shed and then crawled back under the sofa and looked up, there isn't enough room to bang your hammer.

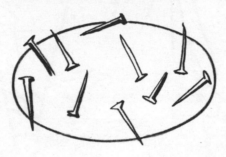

Which meant the nails wouldn't go in properly.

Which meant the flap kept flapping down all over the place again.

Which meant there was only one thing left I could do.

The **trouble with using the big scissors to cut the material under the sofa right off** is it makes you realize what a big piece of material it is.

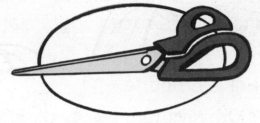

"I think we should go and play on my scooter," said Gabby, scooting across the carpet and heading for my front door.

"I think you're right," I said, rolling up the underneath-sofa material and stuffing it under my T-shirt.

CHAPTER 9

When we got outside on the pavement, we raced right to the top of my road and hid the piece of material in a hedge.

"It's OK. My mum will never know," I said to Gabby, pushing the material a little bit further out of sight.

"But what if she wakes up, goes downstairs into the lounge, turns upside down, lies on her back, crawls under the sofa and looks up??" Gabby asked.

"Why would she ever do that?!" I

asked. "The only thing my mum ever does when she gets up is go into the kitchen, make a cup of coffee and sit on a stool. Sometimes she makes some toast as well, but she never goes into the lounge, lies on her back, crawls under the sofa and looks up. If she did, she would spill her coffee."

Once I'd reassured Gabby that we were never going to get found out, she began to feel a lot better.

"SQUIRTY TIME!" she said, squirting me down the front of my T-shirt and then scooting as fast as she could to the other end of the road.

The **trouble with being squirted with water** is it means you need to fight back.

So I turned into a killer shark. But Gabby said I couldn't because sharks can't live on pavements.

So I turned into a werewolf. But Gabby said werewolves only come out at night.

So I turned into a robot. But Gabby said water makes robots rust.

By the time I had turned into a

zombie mermaid, I was soaked.

"We need to fill up again!" said Gabby, pressing the squirter button as hard as she could, but getting hardly any squirts to squirt at me at all.

The **trouble with filling up again** is we didn't really want to go back into the house, in case my mum was there, lying down on the floor of the lounge, crawling under the sofa and looking up.

And Gabby's house was too far away.

"I know where we can fill up from," I said, taking my turn on the scooter and scooting down the road to the hedge outside Mrs Pike's house.

The **trouble with borrowing someone's hosepipe** is you should really ask first. Trouble is, it was a Sunday morning, it was only about ten o'clock and I was sure Mrs Pike liked having a lie-in just as much as my mum.

Plus, she might have said no.

The hosepipe Mrs Pike had lent Mum to rinse her car with was curled up on a special hosepipe holder right next to her front door. There was an outside water tap just above it with one end of the hosepipe already attached. Which meant all I had to do was turn the tap on, uncurl the hosepipe, poke it under the fence into my garden and then run out of Mrs Pike's garden as fast as I could without being seen.

When I crept into Mrs Pike's front garden, all of her curtains were still drawn so I was almost absolutely

definitely certain that she was still asleep.

It's lucky I'm a really fast runner, because the moment I had uncurled the hosepipe and poked it under the fence, Gabby squealed at me with big bulging eyes and then ducked down.

Can you believe it?! Mrs Pike had opened her bedroom curtains at the exact same time that I was running out of her garden!

As soon as I got through the gate, I dived down onto the pavement and lay down next to Gabby.

"Did she see us?" I panted.

"I don't think so," Gabby gasped.

After about five minutes of lying on the pavement we decided that Mrs Pike couldn't possibly have seen us.

"Let's crawl back to my garden and fill up," I said.

When we got to my gate, we stood up and raced over to the fence.

"Bagsy I fill up first," I said, pulling the squirty end of the hosepipe under the fence and twisting the nozzle with my fingers till the water started to squirt through.

"Bagsy I undo the lid of the water tank," said Gabby, lifting the lid and then standing the scooter up straight so that the maximum amount of water would squirt in.

Squirting water into Gabby's scooter with a hosepipe was really easy, plus there were loads of other things in the garden to squirt as well, like the grass, the flowers, three bumblebees, a spider's web and Gabby's back!

"That's cheating!" squealed Gabby, jumping backwards and running towards the gate. "I'm going to get you for that!"

"Get me all you want!" I laughed. "We've got all the squirts we could ever need!"

CHAPTER 10

The **trouble with having all the squirts you could ever need** is it makes you just want to keep on squirting!

It was about half-past two before Mrs Pike realized that we were using her hosepipe to fill up Gabby's scooter. By then we had already filled up around a hundred times.

We'd played zombie mermaids, zombie sea lions, zombie starfish, zombie penguins, zombie pelicans, zombie otters, zombie lemmings, zombie coastguards and normal

pirates (who turned into zombies after they had dug up a treasure chest full of zombie jewels).

Honestly, Gabby and me had never squirted each other so much in our lives! In fact, by the time Mrs Pike found out that we were using her hosepipe, the squirts had nearly gone right through to our knickers!

I don't know how my mum hadn't noticed we were using the hosepipe before Mrs Pike did. I mean, when she came out into the front garden around eleven to see if I had had any breakfast, she didn't say a thing. Even about us being wet! Mind you, my mum never seems to notice very much at all when she still has her dressing gown on.

When she came outside again around twelve-thirty to give us a plate of sandwiches and some crisps, she still didn't notice Mrs Pike's hosepipe nozzle poking under our fence. Mind you, I think she might have been more interested in getting us some towels.

When Mrs Pike came out of her house for the first time on Sunday, she noticed that we were using her hosepipe straight away. Mostly because she tripped over it as

soon as she stepped out of her front door.

That's the **trouble with hosepipes**. If you stretch them across a front door they can turn into something quite dangerous.

A bit like a trip wire.

Or a booby trap.

Or a zombie trap.

Anyway, as soon as Mrs Pike had picked herself up off her lawn, she went to have a chat with my mum.

Gabby and me were banned from outdoor taps and indoor taps after that.

The **trouble with being banned from outdoor taps and indoor taps** is it means once you run out of water, there is no more water to play with.

Which means you need to make your last tank of water really special.

As soon as we realized we only had one tank of water left to play with, we sat on the pavement outside my gate and wondered how brilliant we could make our very last squirts.

That's when I had the best squirting idea I'd ever had.

"What about if we put some orange in with our water!" I said. "If we pour some orange squash into our water tank and make the water all orangey-tasting, we can aim squirts into our mouths instead of all down our fronts and backs! It'll be brilliant! And thirst-quenching if we're really good with our aims!"

Gabby thought it was a brilliant idea too!

We were banned from orange squash as well after that.

"Think really hard," I said, lying down on the lawn to dry out. "There must be some more ways for me to get the money I need."

But we had run out of ideas.

"I need to go home," said Gabby, peeping over the window ledge to see if my mum had left the lounge. "You can still keep all the money from my piggy bank and I promise I'll start saving up for you again, as soon as I get in."

It was the best and kindest promise Gabby had ever made me.

"Remember, you only need £97.23 more," she said, scooting her scooter towards my garden gate. "I'm sure I will be able to think of an idea that will get you the rest of the money you need!"

"Tell me about it at school

tomorrow!" I said.

"You bet!" said Gabby, holding up her empty piggy bank and waving it.

CHAPTER 11

When I met up with Gabby on the way to school on Monday, we still hadn't thought of any new ways for me to earn £97.23, but she did have her new scooter with her!

Everyone at school thought Gabby's new squirting scooter was immense! Apart from Jack Beechwhistle, because he was the first one who got squirted.

Then he said that his dad was going to be buying him a better type of squirter that would turn Gabby into mincemeat. It was called a "water

cannon". It would be like a tank with a giant squirter on the front that was so immense it could knock you off your feet or pin you to a wall with one squirt.

Nobody believed him, so Gabby squirted him again and then chased him around the playground doing squirts, flashes and alien gargling chipmunk noises.

The **trouble with squirts, flashes and alien gargling chipmunk noises** is it's not only children who can see and hear them, it's teachers too.

As soon as I saw Mrs Allen and Mrs Tompkins running across the playground with frowns on their faces, I knew that Gabby was going to get into trouble. Especially as Jack's friends Colin Kettle and Harry Bayliss had started deliberately on purposely daring Gabby to squirt them too.

The **trouble with someone daring you to squirt them** is it means you HAVE to squirt them.

Even if they've got school uniform on and even if squirting in the playground is against school rules.

If you ask me, most of Gabby's squirts hardly touched Colin, Jack and Harry, because they kept jumping out of the way every time Gabby tried to get them. But she still got into trouble though.

Everyone thought it was really funny when Gabby was made to get off her scooter "this instant" by two cross teachers. Jack, Colin and Harry thought it was hilarious. They even made faces behind the teachers' backs when Gabby was being told off.

As soon as the bell went for morning register and everyone started walking to their classes, I thought Gabby would be allowed to go and park her scooter in the bike sheds. But she wasn't. Mrs Tompkins made her go and park her scooter outside the headmaster's office instead.

Squirting scooters were banned from school after that. And flashing scooters. And scooters that made alien gargling chipmunk noises. Or any other noises. Including squeaky brakes.

When we went back into the playground for morning break on

Monday, Jack Beechwhistle started telling Gabby to do loads of things "this instant". Which was really annoying.

Gabby told Jack that she might not be able to bring her squirting scooter into school any more, but if she ever saw him anywhere near her house after school or on weekends, then she would squirt him on the spot.

Which made Jack want revenge.

The **trouble with revenge** is it can make people say things that are really mean.

And things that don't make sense.
Jack told Gabby that no one
squirted him or any of his friends
and got away with it, so Gabby had
better start watching her back.

The **trouble with watching your back** is it's impossible, because your eyes can't stretch round that far. Unless you're an owl.

Trouble is, before Gabby could prove that watching your back was impossible, the bell went and we had to go back to our lessons.

When we went back into the playground for afternoon break on

Monday, Jack Beechwhistle told Gabby that he was going to drive his water cannon to her house and aim it down her chimney.

The **trouble with aiming a water cannon down a chimney** is it makes your house get flooded. And it makes your toys all wet.

Then Harry and Colin said they were getting water cannons too.

Which meant that now it was three against one.

The **trouble with three against one** is three against one isn't fair. So I told Harry, Jack and Colin that if they wanted to get revenge against Gabby, then they would have to get revenge against me too.

Jack said that if we wanted a war then we should bring it on.

By the time we left school on Monday, I had never wanted or needed a squirting scooter so badly.

Or £97.23.

CHAPTER 12

It was actually Thursday before Gabby came up with her genius idea for getting me all the money I needed. By then our war with Jack, Harry and Colin had kind of fizzled out. Both me and Gabby would still like to have given them all a good squirting, but Gabby wasn't allowed to bring her squirting scooter into school any more, no one was allowed to say the words "squirting" or "scooter" in class any more, plus when we asked Jack Beechwhistle about his water cannon, he said it had got lost in the post.

"A BOOT SALE!" said Gabby, grabbing me by the arm on the way to school on Thursday. "My mum and dad are doing a car boot sale on Sunday. Why don't you come too? We can sell all the things we don't want any more and earn loads of scooter money for you while we're doing it! You could come and stay round my house on Saturday night, plus we could have a sleepover!"

It was the immensest idea ever EVER!

As soon as Gabby asked me to
do a boot sale and a sleepover, I
wrapped my arms around my mum

and asked her if I could go. And guess what? She said YES – as long as it was OK with Gabby's parents. It was so exciting! I'd never done a car boot sale before! I'd never even done a sleepover before!!

How was I ever going to concentrate in class after that?!

The **trouble with concentrating in class** is it's absolutely impossible if the lessons you are doing aren't as exciting as a car boot sale or a sleepover.

When we sat down at our desks after morning assembly, I couldn't think about long division at all. All I could think about was what things I could sell at the boot sale, and what things we could eat for a midnight feast.

"I could sell my Beyblades," I whispered to Gabby, instead of working out 132 divided by 12.

"I could sell my second-best teddy," I whispered to Gabby, instead of working out 126 divided by 9.

"Shall we have smoky-bacon crisps or chicken-flavoured crisps?" I whispered to Gabby, instead of working out 105 divided by 7. "How much do you think I'll get for my three-colour torch?"

The **trouble with whispering to Gabby** is, if you whisper too loud, Mrs Peters will hear you.

The **trouble with Mrs Peters hearing you** is she'll come and have a look at the things you've been writing down.

The **trouble with Mrs Peters looking at what you've been writing down** is I hadn't been writing anything down. At least, not anything to do with long division.

"SEASHELLS?" said Mrs Peters, reading out some of the other things on my list. "ROLLERBLADES? . . . LIGHT-UP YO-YO? . . . CHEESE-AND-HAM SANDWICHES?" (They were for the midnight feast.) "PIGGY BANK?"

The **trouble with seashells, rollerblades, light-up yo-yos, cheese-and-ham sandwiches and piggy banks** is they weren't the answers to any of the sums.

Which meant Mrs Peters got cross.

Which meant I had to go and stand in the corner of the classroom and face the wall. And miss morning break. Which was a bit annoying really. It wasn't until lunch-time break that I was able to properly talk to Gabby about all the things we were going to sell at the boot sale and eat for our midnight feast.

Gabby told me that the best things to sell at a boot sale were expensive things like PlayStations or Xboxes or their games. Then she told me that the best things to have for a midnight feast were sweets.

When I told her that I didn't have an Xbox or a PlayStation, she said it didn't really matter. It was just that the more things are worth at a boot sale, the more money people will pay you for them.

When I asked her about the sweets, she said that the more sweets we could get, the better.

As soon as we'd eaten our packed lunches, we went into the playground and sat on the quiet bench. Quiet benches are totally the best places to concentrate. In fact, I don't know why they don't put quiet benches in classrooms as well.

By the time our lunch-time break was over, we had written two long lists of all the things we could think of to sell at a boot sale, plus a joint list of all the things we could think of to eat and drink at our midnight feast.

This is my list:

MY (DAISY'S) THINGS TO
SELL AT THE BOOT SALE:

Piggy bank
Beyblades
Colouring set (remember to
re-sharpen)
Three-colour torch
Rollerblades
Beano annual
High School Musical jigsaw
Seashells
Snail shells (if I could find any)
Second-favourite teddy
~~First-favourite teddy~~
Big marble
Bendy ruler
School uniform

This is Gabby's list:

MY (GABBY'S) THINGS TO SELL
AT THE BOOT SALE:

PlayStation games
Skipping rope
Telescope
Justin Bieber pencil case
Justin Bieber calendar
Justin Bieber everything
Dream catcher
Swimming goggles
French dictionary
Bike
Barbies
Ken
Snow shaker
Second-best frisbee

This is our midnight feast:

OUR (DAISY AND GABBY'S)
THINGS FOR A MIDNIGHT
FEAST:

Marshmallows
Strawberry Dip Dabs
Fruit pastilles
Mars bars
Maltesers
Chocolate buttons
Chocolate raisins
Chocolate peanuts
Anything that's chocolate
Or with chocolate on
Any fizzy drink
Anything else we can get

Do you know what? I think me and Gabby did more writing on our lists that lunch time than we had in our school books all week! I'm surprised we had any ink left in our pens by the time we'd finished.

And can you blame us? I mean, we were going to be doing an actual sleepover followed by an actual boot sale that very actual weekend!

It was so exciting! It was so immense!

How could I possibly have concentrated on the Battle of Hastings after that?

CHAPTER 13

When my mum talked to Gabby's mum on the way home from school on Thursday afternoon, everything was decided. My mum would drop me off at Gabby's house at five o'clock on

Saturday. I would do a sleepover with Gabby on Saturday night, and then, at five a.m. on Sunday morning, me, Gabby and her mum and dad would get up and drive to the car boot sale with all the things we had to sell.

Five a.m. in the MORNING!!!

I'd never been up that early before in my whole life! (Apart from to go to Spain on holiday!)

Things got even better when my mum invited Gabby and her mum and dad round to our house after the boot sale for a late Sunday dinner.

Gabby's mum said that they would need some time after the boot sale to unload the car again and to take anything they hadn't sold to the charity shop.

"Is four o'clock OK for Sunday lunch, then?" asked my mum.

"Four o'clock it is!" said Gabby's mum.

As soon as our mums had done the arrangements, I started to get even more excited about going to the boot sale.

The instant I got home from school I ran upstairs to my bedroom, got changed and then started putting all the things I was going to sell into one big box.

"How much do you think I will get if I sell all these?" I asked, giving my mum my list.

The **trouble with giving your mum a list** is, if it's a boot sale list, she will start trying to make you think that you are selling some of the wrong things.

"You can't sell your piggy bank!" she said. "Your nanny and grampy bought that for you when you were little!"

"There's never anything in it!" I said.

"Are you sure you want to sell your rollerblades?" she said. "You've only had them a year."

"I won't need rollerblades if I've got a new squirting scooter!" I said.

Mum said that I should think very carefully about all the things I was going to take to the boot sale, because once I had sold them, I wouldn't be able to get them back.

When I told her that I needed to earn £97.23 and that I was bound to get at least £50 for my rollerblades, she gave me a very funny look.

"I think you might find that people who go to car boot sales won't want to pay as much as you want them to pay," she said.

"They will when they see what I'm selling," I said.

"Why are you selling your seashells?" she asked. "You love those seashells. You bought them at the airport in Spain."

When I told her that if you put your ear to a Spanish seashell, the sound of the sea is in the wrong language, she told me I was being silly.

"Daisy," she said, "I know how much you would like to have a scooter just like Gabby's, but selling all your toys is a very drastic way of going about it. Toys are part of your childhood, toys are part of growing up, toys are special. I wish I had kept some of the toys I played with as a child."

I didn't even know toys were invented when my mum was a child. In fact, I'm not sure my mum was ever a child. At least, not a proper child like me and Gabby.

When I told her that my second-favourite teddy had been giving me funny looks for no reason, she said that was no reason to sell a teddy at all.

When I told her that my light-up yo-yo kept going up when it was meant to go down, she said that this had nothing to do with the yo-yo and everything to do with me. Which is a lie.

Honestly, whose toys were they anyway!?! Not my mum's! MINE!!

By the time I'd put my pyjamas on, cleaned my teeth and got into bed on Thursday, the only thing my mum had actually forced me to take out of my box was my school uniform.

"IF YOU THINK YOU ARE SELLING YOUR SCHOOL UNIFORM AT A CAR BOOT SALE, DAISY, YOU CAN THINK AGAIN!" she said.

So I did think again.

I thought again all through breakfast, all the way to school and all through lessons in class on Friday.

CHAPTER 14

I was still thinking when my mum came to tuck me in on Friday night as well!

"Daisy, you are NOT selling your bed!" said my mum when she came into my bedroom and found me lying on the floor.

When I told her that I had decided to sleep on the carpet from now on, she still said no.

Mum said I wasn't allowed to sell my bed, my pillows, my duvet, my bedside table, my bedside lamp or anything else to do with my bed.

She wouldn't even let me sell my bedroom curtains.

"But I need £97.23!" I said. "If people at the boot sale won't want to pay as much as I want them to pay, how am I going to earn £97.23?!"

When I asked if I could sell my bedroom door because I always keep it open, Mum said that she was beginning to wish she'd never said yes to a car boot sale. But I knew that wasn't true, because I had already heard her arranging to go to the cinema with Mrs Pike on Saturday night.

That's how parents work. As soon as they realize that you are not going to be around, they arrange to have loads of fun themselves. Plus, I knew that she was really looking forward to an extra long lie-in on Sunday too.

So I asked her if I could sell my wardrobe.

The **trouble with selling your wardrobe** is it leaves you nowhere to hang your clothes.

So I offered to sell my clothes too. (Not including my school uniform.)

But Mum still wouldn't let me put anything extra in my box. (Not that the wardrobe would have fitted.)

All she did was kiss me goodnight and tell me to "THINK AGAIN!" again.

So I did think again, again.

I thought again right up till I fell asleep on Friday, right through breakfast on Saturday morning and all the way up to the moment I put the milk back in the fridge.

"How much would people pay for a piece of ham?" I asked.

"People wouldn't pay anything for

a piece of ham," sighed Mum.

"They would if they were hungry,"
I said. "If they're going to a boot sale
and they've forgotten to have any
breakfast, a piece of ham could be

just what they need. Six pieces of ham would be even better."

"We need the ham for our sandwiches at lunch time, Daisy," said Mum.

"How much would people pay for ten Rice Krispies?" I asked. "Or fifty Rice Krispies? If I put fifty Rice Krispies into bags, fill the bags up with milk and sell them as take-away breakfasts at the boot sale, I'll make a fortune!"

"You'll make a mess," said Mum.

"Is there anything in the shed I could sell?" I asked.

"Only cobwebs," said Mum.

"Is there anything in the loft I could sell?"

"Only cobwebs," said Mum.

"Do we need that toaster?" I asked.

"YES!" she growled.

"Then you leave me no choice," I said, running to the phone to tell Gabby about my new emergency plan.

When I told Gabby that I was going to be selling my favourite teddy at the boot sale, she did a really loud gasp on the phone. "YOUR FAVOURITE TEDDY!" she squeaked. "I would never sell my favourite teddy, not for all the money in the world!"

Trouble is, she was already the lucky owner of a squirting scooter that did flashes and really cool noises, so it was easy for her to say that.

"But if I sell my favourite teddy, I might get £97.23 for it!" I said. "If I get £97.23 for it, I won't have to sell any of my other things."

But Gabby still kept doing loads of gasps. "I think the idea of taking something special to sell at a boot sale is a really good one, Daisy," she said, "but I would only sell my favourite teddy if I was really, really desperate. I mean, like, if my whole life depended on it. Why don't you take your favourite teddy, keep him out of sight, see how much you get for all the ordinary things you are selling, and if you get desperate . . ."

"Sell my teddy?" I said.

"Exactly," said Gabby. "But only if you are desperate."

It was really good advice because I actually didn't want to sell my favourite teddy at all.

"You do know that if you sell your favourite teddy, you will never see him again, don't you?" said Gabby.

"That's what my mum said," I told her.

"If I was you, I'd keep thinking," said Gabby.

"REALLY?" I sighed.

I don't think I'd ever thought so much in my life.

CHAPTER 15

When I arrived at Gabby's house on Saturday, I had absolutely everything I needed. I had my box of things to sell

at the boot sale, I had my sleeping bag, my pyjamas, my toothbrush, my favourite teddy, plus all the things we needed for our midnight feast!

Well, some of the things.

"I only managed to get chocolate raisins," I said as we went upstairs to Gabby's bedroom, "and two strawberry Dip Dabs."

"No problem," said Gabby. "My mum and dad have bought us stacks of sweets to eat!"

"Where shall I put them?" I asked.

"Hide them under our pillows," said Gabby, "and then we'll go back downstairs and get some more

sweets for our secret stash!"

By the time we'd added a king-sized bottle of lemonade, a big bag of marshmallows, a box of Maltesers, some Cheestrings, a bunch of bananas, two sausage rolls, a family packet of cheesy Wotsits, a packet of Love Hearts, some Candy Sticks and  a box of jam tarts to our secret stash, it didn't look that secret at all. Because the pillows were so high.

So we put the bananas back.

Gabby said that the more midnight feast we ate, the more our pillows would go down. Trouble is, it wasn't midnight. It was time for proper dinner.

The **trouble with having proper dinner with Gabby AND her mum and dad** is they all like peas.

And I don't.

Which was a bit of a problem really, because when I sat down at the table, Gabby's mum gave me a plate with peas all over it.

The **trouble with having a plate with peas all over it** is I really, really don't like peas.

Especially baby peas, because you get more of them.

The **trouble with saying I don't like peas** is it's a bit embarrassing if you're saying it to someone else's mum. Especially if they are letting you do a sleepover in their house AND taking you to a boot sale the next day.

So I tried to pretend that I did.

The **trouble with pretending to like peas** is you have to put a pea in your mouth.

The **trouble with putting a pea in your mouth** is it makes your tongue shrink.

And your teeth faint.

And your mouth dry up.

Which is why I had to spit it out.

I don't think Gabby's mum and dad were very pleased when I did my spit.

"Is something wrong, Daisy?!" asked Gabby's mum. "You haven't found a hair in your dinner, have you?"

"She doesn't like peas," said Gabby.

Luckily, as soon as Gabby's mum found out I didn't like peas, she scraped all my peas onto Gabby's dad's plate instead.

Including the one I spat out.

"Sorry," I whispered to Gabby.

"It's OK," she whispered back. "I don't like courgettes."

Whatever they are.

As soon as we had finished our shepherd's pie, Gabby asked if we could leave the table.

Gabby's dad said that there was dessert if we wanted it, but we were both really keen to go back to Gabby's room.

"We're going to put our pyjamas on!" said Gabby. "In fact, we're going to go to bed right now! Is it all right if Daisy sleeps in my bed with me? Can she, can she, can she?!?"

It was only half-past six, but we'd never been so keen to go to bed in our whole lives!

"Of course she can," said Gabby's mum. "But remember, we are getting up at **five o'clock**!"

CHAPTER 16

As soon as we got back to Gabby's bedroom, I dived straight into my bag for my pyjamas.

"Leave your sleeping bag on the floor!" said Gabby. "There's plenty of room in my bed for both of us!"

Gabby was right. Her bed was a double bed, which made it twice as wide as mine (same length, though). Twice as long would have been even better!

"Ta-da!" said Gabby, jumping into bed first and then lifting both pillows

to reveal our midnight feast.

The **trouble with midnight feasts** is they are really meant to start at midnight.

So once we'd both got under the covers, we decided we would have a quarter-to-seven feast instead. Trouble is it was only twenty to seven. So we changed it to a twenty-to-seven feast instead, because we hadn't had any dessert.

The **trouble with dessert** is, if you're sitting at a dinner table, you only get one choice of things to eat.

But if you're sitting in bed with Gabby having an early midnight feast, there are absolutely loads of things you can have!

Gabby fancied cheesy Wotsits, Love Hearts and lemonade for her dessert. I fancied chocolate raisins, a Dip Dab, some Maltesers and a jam tart. Then Gabby changed her mind.

So I changed my mind too.

In the end we decided to open everything and just eat whatever we fancied when we fancied it.

It was brilliant fun being in the same bed as Gabby. I'd never been under the covers with anyone before, apart from my mum, and Gabby was loads more fun!

"Let's pretend we are moles!"
she said, crawling under the covers
towards the other end of the bed.

"Let's pretend we're in a tunnel, looking for worms to eat, but the only things we can find are cheesy Wotsits!"

So we did!

"Let's pretend we're trapped in a cave!" said Gabby, lying on her back and holding the duvet up with her feet.

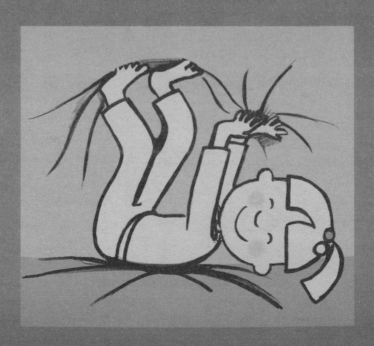

"Let's pretend we were digging for diamonds but the roof has collapsed and now we have to dig our way out of all the boulders!"

So we did!

Once we'd cleared all the boulders, I began to have sleepover ideas of my own.

"Let's pretend we're robbing a bank!" I said, lying flat on my tummy and wriggling like a snake.

"Let's pretend we are digging a tunnel under a bank and our tunnel leads straight to a safe that is full of £97.23!"

"How are we going to get the safe open?" asked Gabby, wriggling along next to me.

"We can pick the lock with a Cheestring!" I said.

Having a sleepover with Gabby was IMMENSE! The more under-the-covers adventures we had, the sillier they became. The sillier they became, the louder we began to giggle.

"Let's pretend we're the insides of a tortoise and the duvet is our shell!"

I giggled.

"That's WEIRD!!" giggled Gabby.

"No, this is WEIRD!" I laughed, stuffing my cheeks with marsh-mallows and poking four Candy Sticks up my nose.

Honestly, I never knew there were so many things you could do under the covers with a midnight feast! By the time we decided to come out to get some air, it was as dark outside the covers as it was under them!

"What time is it?" asked Gabby when her mum poked her head round the door.

"Time you two stopped giggling and went to sleep," she said.

"But it's a sleepover!" laughed Gabby.

"I know," said her mum. "Time to concentrate on the SLEEP bit. *Comprende*?"

"*Comprende,*" sighed Gabby.

"So no more giggling?" asked Gabby's mum.

"No more giggling," nodded Gabby.

"Promise?" said Gabby's mum.

"We promise!" we fibbed.

CHAPTER 17

The **trouble with promising not to giggle** is it makes you giggle.

As soon as Gabby's mum closed the door, our giggles started again straight away. So we had to go back under the duvet again to make them sound quieter.

"I didn't know you could speak Spanish," I whispered.

"I can't," giggled Gabby. *"Comprende* is the only Spanish word I know."

The **trouble with making up other words in Spanish** is it made us giggle more. Especially *sleepovero.*

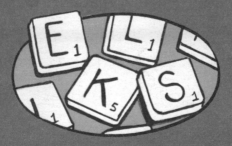

So we changed countries.

The trouble with making up words in Eskimo is it made us giggle just as much.

Especially *pigloo*. Gabby said a *pigloo* was a house where Eskimo pigs live, but I said it was the place where little Eskimo pigs went for a *weeee weeeee weeeee all the way home*!

Which made us giggle so much we both had to go for a wee of our own!

When we tiptoed across the landing to the bathroom, we saw that all the lights had been turned off downstairs, which meant Gabby's mum and dad had actually gone to bed too. Which meant it was even later than we thought!

But we still couldn't stop giggling when we got back into bed.

The **trouble with thinking of names to call Jack Beechwhistle** is it made us giggle.

The **trouble with thinking of things to put in Mrs Peters' desk** is it made us giggle.

The **trouble with tickling each other with sweet wrappers** is it made us giggle.

We just couldn't stop ourselves. Until Gabby did a fart in the bed.

The **trouble with Gabby doing a fart in the bed** is it made me desperate get out from under the covers as fast as I could!!!!

The **trouble with getting out from under the covers as fast as I could** is it made me fall out of bed and onto the floor. Which made us both giggle till we burst.

Which is why Gabby's bedroom door opened again.

Only this time it wasn't Gabby's mum, it was her dad!

Which meant it was serious.

"Girls, will you PLEASE quieten down," he said. "We all have to get up really early tomorrow morning and if we don't get any sleep, we'll be fit for nothing."

"We promise," we proper promised this time.

The **trouble with proper promising not to giggle** is it makes your sleepover go really quiet.

And the room seem even darker when the door closes.

"I'm just going to get my teddy out of my bag," I whispered. "In case he's afraid of going to sleep in a strange bedroom."

"I guess this might be the last time you ever sleep with your favourite teddy again," said Gabby with a huge yawn.

"I hope not," I whispered, climbing back into bed. "I really, really hope not."

As soon as I got back under the covers, I made teddy comfortable on the pillow next to my cheek.

"Do you think we should clean our teeth?" I whispered.

But there was no answer.

There wasn't even a giggle.

Or even a fart.

Can you believe it? Gabby had only gone and fallen asleep!

CHAPTER 18

When Gabby and I were woken up
on Sunday morning, my eyelids felt
like they were glued together.

"It's five o'clock," said Gabby's mum, knocking and then poking her head round Gabby's door.

"It's too early," groaned Gabby, hiding her head under her pillow.

To start with, I thought it was too early too, but after I'd done a few blinks and rubbed my eyes, I got my eyelids working again.

"Gabby, we need to get up," I said, pulling the pillow off her face. "It's time to go to the boot sale. Come on. Get up. It's going to be immense!"

After about twenty more blinks and six or seven more groans, Gabby rolled out of bed. By about twenty past five, we were both dressed and ready go.

Trouble is, we had to have breakfast.

The **trouble with having to have breakfast** is egg and bacon can be really hard to eat if you're still full up with midnight feast. Especially when there's baked beans and toast on your plate too.

Luckily, Gabby's dad was really hungry so we only had to have a piece of toast.

Because Gabby's dad's had loaded up the car with all the boot sale things the night before, all we had to do was wash our faces, clean our teeth, go to the loo, get my teddy, get in and put our seat belts on.

By about ten to six we were on the road!

I'd never sat in the smell of a brand-new car before. It smelled all lovely and new car-ey.

"Where's all the traffic?" I asked as we drove away from Gabby's house onto a really empty road.

"Still asleep in their garages," yawned Gabby.

"Anyone you see on the road at this time, Daisy, will probably be going to the boot sale," said Gabby's dad.

"Really?" I said, deciding that from then on I was going to count cars.

By the time we arrived at the boot sale entrance, I had worked out there would be at least thirty-seven cars going to the boot sale. When we actually drove in through the entrance, I couldn't believe my eyes! There were hundreds of cars already lined up in the field, and loads more queuing to get in!

Once Gabby's dad had paid some money, he drove us to our boot sale spot and parked the car.

"OK, everyone," said Gabby's mum, undoing her seat belt and looking round at us with a smile, "let's get set up!"

The **trouble with setting up** is as soon as you open the back of your car, strangers start crowding round and peering in to see what you've got inside. Which makes it really difficult to get things out.

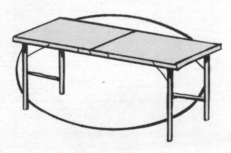

Gabby's mum and dad had brought a clothes rail and two wallpaper-pasting tables to put their things on. Trouble is, they couldn't get to them.

"I'm not selling anything to anyone

until I've had a chance to set up our stall!" said Gabby's dad, getting a bit cross with a very nosy man. "If you don't leave us alone for ten minutes, I will turn the car round and go home!"

Which was a lie. But it worked! At least, it worked when he closed the boot of the car again and folded his arms.

"OK, let's do this," said Gabby's dad, opening the car again as the nosy people began walking away.

Once we'd got the tables set up, all we had to do was put the things we were selling on top. Gabby's mum and dad had given Gabby and me our own table to share. The things we were selling looked absolutely brilliant by the time we had finished setting them out.

"Don't forget to hide your favourite teddy," said Gabby.

"Don't worry," I said, "I've left him at the bottom of my boot sale box."

"Good luck!" she said, crossing her fingers. "And remember to only sell him if you get desperate."

"I will," I said, crossing my fingers too. "Or rather, I won't!"

CHAPTER 19

When the boot sale opened at seven o'clock, people started walking past our table from all directions.

But that was the problem. Everyone kept walking past and not stopping.

"Why aren't they stopping?" I whispered to Gabby.

"I don't think we've got anything they want to buy," she whispered back.

"They're buying things from your mum and dad," I said.

"Mum and Dad are mostly selling

clothes," said Gabby. "Grown-ups like buying clothes at boot sales."

"They still aren't stopping," I said after about five minutes. "Some of them aren't even looking."

The **trouble with people not even looking** is it made me get cross. Which is why I started giving people my special stares.

"Be patient," said Gabby, moving her French dictionary to the front of the table and then putting her snow shaker in front of her second-best frisbee. "Someone will come along soon."

The **trouble with being patient** is it makes me really impatient. Especially when people who are meant to come along soon don't come along soon enough.

"What's the matter with everyone?" I said to Gabby as about six more

grown-ups walked straight past us. "IS EVERYONE BLIND?" I said in a probably bit too loud voice.

Still, at least it made them look.

"Here come some children!" said Gabby, tugging me by the arm and then telling me to "act casual".

Gabby was right: an actual boy and an actual girl were coming straight towards us with their parents!

"How much is this?" said the boy, stopping beside our table and picking up my big marble.

"£55," I said, getting ready to put it into a bag.

"Oh," he said, putting it back on the table and walking away.

"How much is this seashell?" asked the girl, picking up my favourite seashell.

"Are you Spanish or English?" I asked.

"I'm English," she said.

"Then it's £45," I said. "It would be £60 if you were Spanish, because the sea sounds work much better in Spanish."

"Oh," said the girl, putting the seashell down and walking away.

Can you believe it? They both WALKED AWAY!

"I think you're asking for too much money," whispered Gabby, dropping something into a bag and giving it to a boy that I hadn't even seen approaching.

"What have you sold!?" I asked.

"My Ken," Gabby said.

"How much for?" I asked.

"20p," she told me.

When Gabby told me that she'd sold an actual Ken with all his actual Ken clothes on for only 20p, I nearly fainted.

"20p?!" I said. "An actual Ken is worth more than 20p!

His trousers must be worth more than 20p. How can you sell anything for 20p?!"

"Pretty easily," said Gabby, moving her snow shaker nearer her swimming goggles, "because 20p is about what people at boot sales want to pay."

When Gabby told me how mean people were at boot sales, I nearly wanted to put everything back in my box.

"How much do you think I should have asked for my big marble?" I asked.

"About 10p," she said.

"BUT IT'S MASSIVE!" I said.

"I know," she said, "but it's a boot sale."

"How much do you think I should have asked for my seashell?" I asked.

"About 50p," she said.

"And what if the person buying it was Spanish?" I asked.

"About 50p," she said.

For about the next three minutes, I couldn't even give people my special stare I was so cross.

"I think we need to have a little talk," said Gabby.

"What about?" I asked.

"Haggling," said Gabby.

CHAPTER 20

The **trouble with haggling** is, instead of people trying to haggle the price up, they try and haggle the price down.

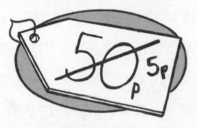

"Everyone haggles at a boot sale," said Gabby. "Basically, the way haggling works is you decide what price you want to sell something for, then you add 50p, so that when someone asks you the price of the thing you are selling, you tell them it's 50p more than you want so that they can haggle you down by offering you, say, £1 less, but because you've already added 50p more than you really wanted, you can haggle them back up by saying you want 50p more than the £1 less they are trying to haggle you down to, so in the end the price you haggle them back up to might be 50p less than you said, but it's still 50p more than they said, which is perfect because 50p more than they said is exactly the price you wanted all along! Simple!!"

Well, it was simple to Gabby.

"So how much did you say you wanted for Ken?" I asked.

"£1," said Gabby.

"But how much did you really want for him?"

"50p," said Gabby.

"Then how come you only got 20p for him?" I said.

"Because that boy was a really good haggler," said Gabby. "If people are really good hagglers, then you'll never get the price you want. Unless you're a really good haggler too."

I didn't know if I was going to be a really good haggler at all. All I knew was, there was absolutely no way I was going to be selling any of my things for 20p!

As the sun got hotter and the boot sale got busier, more and more children started to walk towards our table. Even better, most of them stopped to see what Gabby and I had for sale.

"So basically, I think of a price and add 50p?" I whispered to Gabby.

"Basically, yes," said Gabby.

So I did.

"How much are your rollerblades?" asked a girl with a wonky fringe.

"£84.50," I said.

"That's too much," whispered Gabby.

"£49.50," I said.

"That's still too much," whispered Gabby.

"£20.50," I said.

"Still too much," said Gabby.

"Ask Gabby," I said.

The **trouble with asking Gabby** is Gabby has absolutely no idea how good my rollerblades are, because she's never even tried them on!

"£2.50," said Gabby, picking up an empty carrier bag and giving me a secret wink.

"Can I have them for 20p?" asked the girl.

"NO YOU CAN'T!" I said.

"Oh," said the girl, walking away.

Honestly, what is wrong with boot sale people? A boy with crumbs round his mouth wanted to buy my bendy ruler for 5p, a girl chewing bubble gum wanted to buy my three-colour torch for 10p, a boy in a too-big T-shirt wanted all my Beyblades for 3p (because that's all he had left), and three different girls wanted to buy my second-favourite teddy for under £60! I had never met so many mean people in my entire life!!!!!

Gabby didn't seem to mind people being mean at all. She sold her PlayStation games for 50p each, her three Justin Bieber things for £1, her swimming goggles for 20p, her French dictionary for 15p and her skipping rope for I don't know what because I was haggling, her snow shaker for I don't know how much because I was haggling and her second-best frisbee for I have no

idea whatsoever – because guess
what, I was haggling again!

When Gabby's mum came over
to see how we were doing, I didn't
know what to say.

"How much have you made?" she asked.

"I haven't counted yet!" said Gabby.

"Nothing," I mumbled.

The **trouble with nothing** is, when you take it away from £97.23, you are still left with £97.23.

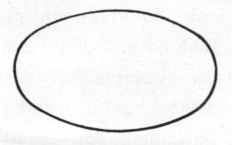

Which meant I was no closer to being able to afford a squirting scooter than I was the day before.

"You shouldn't keep asking so much money for things," said Gabby.

"And you shouldn't keep selling your things for so little when I'm trying to sell my things for what they are worth," I said, "because if people hear how cheap your things are, they are never going to buy my things."

If Gabby hadn't been my best friend, I would probably have given her one of my stares. But I didn't.

"Try doing what I do," said Gabby. "Keep rearranging your toys so they don't always look the same."

So I did. I put my *High School Musical* jigsaw in front of my seashells. I stood my three-colour torch on its end. I put my colouring set next to my second-favourite teddy and I put my piggy bank right in the middle.

But people still didn't want to pay more than 20p!

"Why not just sell one thing for 20p to see how it feels," said Gabby. "I know 20p doesn't sound like very much, but if you get lots of them they can soon add up!"

So I did. I didn't want to. But I did. I sold my piggy bank for 20p to a lady who collects pigs.

The **trouble with selling my piggy bank for 20p** is that now I had 20p, I didn't have anything to put it in. I wanted to kick the table over after that.

"20p!" I humphed. "My whole piggy bank for 20p! It must be worth loads more than that!"

"I know, but it's a boot sale," said Gabby, putting two Barbies into a bag and giving them to a girl for 10p each. "Don't worry, there's still plenty of time."

But there wasn't still plenty of time at all. It was already half-past nine, and by nearly half-past eleven, my piggy bank was still the only thing I had sold. By a quarter to twelve, some people had even started packing their stalls away.

There was only one thing I could do.

It was time to get desperate.

CHAPTER 21

The **trouble with getting desperate** is it makes you do things you know you shouldn't really do. Like sell your favourite teddy.

Or your mum's jewellery without asking.

I had meant to ask my mum if I could take her jewellery box with me to the boot sale, but I'd spent so much time thinking again and again on Saturday, it was the one thing I'd kind of forgotten to think about.

When I walked back to the car and reached down right to the very bottom of my boot sale box, Gabby guessed exactly what I was doing. Well, nearly exactly.

"You're not going to sell your favourite teddy, are you?" she gasped.

"No way," I said, coming back with my mum's jewellery box and putting it on the table in between my big marble and my bendy ruler.

When Gabby saw it, her mouth dropped open like a giant goldfish. "I didn't know you had a jewellery box!" she gasped.

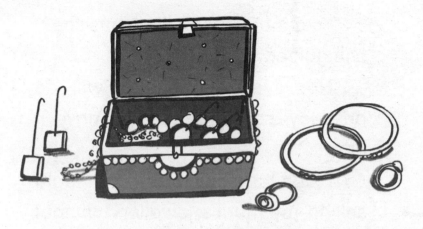

"I don't," I said. "Well, I do and I
don't."

When I explained to Gabby that
the jewellery box was my mum's, but
actually it kind of belonged to me,
because my mum had told me that
when she died she would be leaving
it to me in her will, Gabby's mouth
dropped open even wider.

"Your mum hasn't died, has she?" she gulped.

"No," I said, "but she will do one day, so I may as well have it now."

I don't think Gabby thought selling my mum's jewellery without asking was a very good idea, but she soon changed her mind when I sold a ring and a bracelet to a lady for £35, who then decided she would buy another bracelet for £20, who then decided she would buy the whole jewellery box and everything in it, right there and then, for – wait for it . . .

£125!!!!!

Not 50p or 20p or 10p or 3p, but £125!

It was a deal!

When I asked the lady if she wanted a bag, she said she already had one,  which made it an even better deal! I'd never been so pleased with myself in my whole life.

"I wish I'd brought my mum's jewellery box to sell," said Gabby as we started to pack our table away.

"No need!" I said. "I've got all the money we could ever want!"

When Gabby's mum and dad found out how much I had earned at the boot sale, they were really surprised.

"Goodness! You *have* done well," they said.

"I know!" I said. "Thanks ever so much for bringing me!"

By the time our tables and the clothes rail were folded up and everything was put back in the car, I was nearly wetting myself with excitement.

"You know what this means, don't you, Gabby," I said. "This means it's double-squirt time! Because soon we'll both have a squirting scooter of our very own! In fact, if your dad drives me home right now, I could go to the scooter shop with my mum as soon as I get in and buy a squirting scooter this very afternoon!! Will your dad drive me home right now, WILL HE, WILL HE, WILL HE?! You can bring all my other things back later when you come round for Sunday lunch!"

I knew it was a good plan. Gabby knew it was a good plan.

And after lots of WILL YOU, WILL YOU, WILL YOUS, Gabby's dad said yes!

CHAPTER 22

When my mum heard that I had made
£125.20 at the boot sale, she was
even more surprised than Gabby's
mum and dad.

"Can we go to the scooter shop?" I
begged. "CAN WE, CAN WE, CAN WE?!"

At first my mum didn't seem too
keen. Her eyes looked really red and
bleary, which meant she had probably
been to a wine bar as well as a cinema
with Mrs Pike on Saturday night.

But there was no way I was
going to wait another minute to buy

my squirting scooter.

"PLEASE, PLEASE, PLEASE, MUM," I begged. "I SO, SO, SO WANT A SQUIRTING SCOOTER LIKE GABBY'S!"

"Anything for a quiet life," sighed Mum.

"LET'S GO, LET'S GO, LET'S GO!" I said, racing back to the car, putting my seat belt on for a third time and then bouncing up and down in my seat.

"Calm down, calm down, calm down," said Mum. "Saying everything three times isn't going to get us there any faster!"

"YES IT IS, YES IT IS, YES IT IS!" I laughed.

"No it isn't, no it isn't," sighed Mum. (I think she was too bleary to do three.)

When we got to the scooter shop, I couldn't get out of the car quick enough. I had a big, fat £125.20 in my pocket, but it didn't weigh me down one bit.

"See you in there!" I said, throwing open the door of the car, racing

across the pavement and charging
into the shop.

When I got inside the shop, all I could think about was a squirting scooter. And THERE IT WAS, right in the middle of all the new bikes on a display stand all of its own!

The squirting scooter on the display stand was even newer than Gabby's, which meant it was even shinier than Gabby's too!

"I'd like that squirting scooter please!" I said, sprinting over to the shop counter and jumping up and down.

"LOOK, LOOK, LOOK!" I shouted to my mum as she came into the shop. "LOOK AT THE SCOOTER I'M GETTING!"

"Sorry," Mum said to the shop lady. "She's a little over-excited."

"That's OK," said the shop lady. "It's a very popular scooter."

I hadn't really taken much notice of the lady behind the counter. It was only when I went to pay that

I realized who she was.

By then it was too late.

"They're nice earrings," said Mum as the lady picked up my money. "I've got a pair just like that at home."

"Thank you," said the shop lady. "I only bought them this morning."

"That's a lovely necklace," said Mum as the lady started to count out my £99.99. "I've  got a necklace just like that too!"

"Thank you," said the shop lady.

"I bought the necklace this morning too!"

The **trouble with realizing who someone is too late** is there was nothing I could do.

"Could I have a closer look at your lovely ring?" asked Mum as the lady held out my change. "It so reminds me of a ring I inherited from my grandmother."

"Beautiful, isn't it?" said the shop

lady, lifting her finger up for Mum to admire. "There are three diamonds and a sapphire. Would you believe I bought it at a car boot sale this morning too? In fact," said the shop lady, looking me straight in the eye, "wasn't it you I bought them from?"

The **trouble with going really hot in a bike shop** is it makes you need to run outside straight away to get some fresh air.

Trouble is, Mum had hold of my collar. Really tight.

I decided I didn't actually want to buy a squirting scooter after that.

CHAPTER 23

If Gabby and her mum and dad hadn't been coming round for Sunday lunch later that day, I think Mum would have sent me straight to my bedroom when we got home.

Or prison.

Mum nearly had a fight with the lady in the bike shop, because the lady didn't want to give Mum her jewellery back. Or her jewellery box.

In the end, Mum told the shop lady that if she didn't give her her jewellery back, she was going to ring the police and report her for handling stolen goods. Plus she said that if she didn't get everything back "this instant", she would knock over every bike in the shop.

Luckily the lady lived above the shop, so she only had to go upstairs to get the jewellery box.

Trouble is, then I had to give the £125 back as well.

On the way home in the car, Mum stopped being bleary and changed to being really, really, really, really cross instead. And all because of a silly old jewellery box.

"HOW COULD YOU DO IT, DAISY!" she said. "HOW COULD YOU, HOW COULD YOU, HOW COULD YOU, HOW COULD YOU?!!!!"

When I told her that saying things four times was worse than saying things three times, she got even crosser. When I told her I didn't think any of her jewellery suited her, she nearly crashed the car.

I was so relieved when Gabby and her mum and dad finally came over to our house for Sunday lunch. Because my mum had to pretend she wasn't cross with me, even though she was.

Gabby's dad carried my boot sale box in from the car, and while I was putting all my toys back in my bedroom, I told Gabby what had happened at the bike shop. I gave her her piggy-bank money back too.

"Oh well," said Gabby, "at least you've still got your favourite teddy."

"And all my other things," I said. (Not including my piggy bank.)

Trouble is, when we went back downstairs, everything went wrong for me again.

The lunch went all right – in fact Sunday lunch was really nice, because my midnight feast had totally gone down and I was feeling really hungry again. I even ate some broccoli. It was after Sunday lunch that things got a bit tricky.

The **trouble with boot sales** is, just because you are selling things, it doesn't mean you can't buy things as well.

Gabby's mum told my mum that when things got a bit quiet at the boot sale, she had slipped away to have a browse around some of the other stalls.

Trouble is, while she was browsing, she'd found something that she thought we all might enjoy playing after lunch.

It was a game called Twister.

The **trouble with Twister** is it's a game that everyone can play.

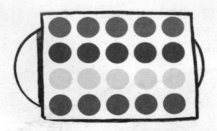

Another **trouble with Twister** is it's a game you have to play on the floor.

The **trouble with floors** is they have sofas on them. So if you're playing Twister in the lounge by the sofa, you might end up on the floor, turning upside down, lying on your back and looking up.

I think you can guess the rest.

"DAISY!"

DAISY'S
TROUBLE INDEX

The trouble with . . .

 Piggy banks 1

 Putting money in a piggy bank 3

 Suddenly needing your money
again 3

 Aliens crossed with chipmunks
crossed with gargling frogs 7

 Seeing your best friend on an
immense squirting micro-scooter 14

 Waking my mum up when she's
sunbathing 16

 Knowing the answer to a question
but not actually hearing it 18

Chores 27

 Being bored 28

 Fruit bowls 29

 Immense sucking, whining, hoovering noises 30

 Washing the dishes 32

 Realizing how hard mashed potato is to get off 33

 Car washing 35

 Using a metal scouring pad 35

 Opening a zoo 40

 Starting a pet hairdresser's 41

Becoming a gold miner 42

 Winning the lottery 42

 Inventing a new invention that everyone in the world would want to buy 43

 Counting up piggy-bank money 52

 Foreign coins 53

 Waking Mum again 57

 Shaking my mum as hard as I could 58

 Taking £2.76 away from £99.99 62

 The underneath of sofas 65

Scissors 66

 Cutting all you can cut and looking all you can look 68

 Sellotape 70

 Nails 71

 Using the big scissors to cut the material under the sofa right off 73

 Being squirted with water 76

 Filling up again 77

 Borrowing someone's hosepipe 78

 Having all the squirts you could ever need 86

Hosepipes 91

 Being banned from outdoor taps
and indoor taps 94

 Squirts, flashes and alien
gargling chipmunk noises 103

 Someone daring you to squirt
them 106

 Revenge 109

 Watching your back 111

 Aiming a water cannon down a
chimney 112

 Three against one 113

Concentrating in class 117

 Whispering to Gabby 119

 Mrs Peters hearing you 120

 Mrs Peters looking at what you've been writing down 120

 Seashells 121

 Rollerblades 121

 Light-up yo-yos 121

 Cheese-and-ham sandwiches 121

 Piggy banks 121

 Giving your mum a list 135

Selling your wardrobe 145

 Having proper dinner with Gabby AND her mum and dad 160

 Having a plate with peas all over it 160

 Saying I don't like peas 161

 Pretending to like peas 161

 Putting a pea in your mouth 162

 Midnight feasts 169

 Dessert 170

 Promising not to giggle 181

Making up other words in Spanish 183

 Making up words in Eskimo 184

 Thinking of names to call Jack Beechwhistle 186

 Thinking of things to put in Mrs Peters' desk 187

 Tickling each other with sweet wrappers 187

 Gabby doing a fart in the bed 188

 Getting out from under the covers as fast as I could 188

Proper promising not to giggle 190

 Having to have breakfast 198

 Setting up 206

 People not even looking 214

 Being patient 215

 Haggling 225

 Asking Gabby 231

 Nothing 235

 Selling my piggy bank for 20p 239

 Getting desperate 241

Realizing who someone is too
late 264

 Going really hot in a bike shop 268

 Boot sales 275

 Twister 276

 Twister 277

 Floors 277

More than a million

DAISY

books sold!

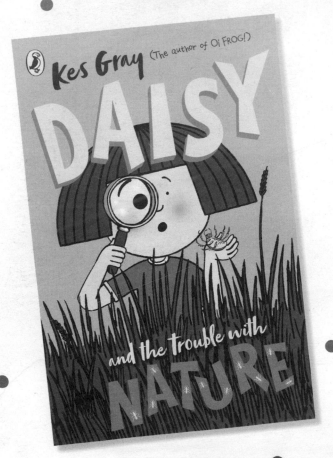